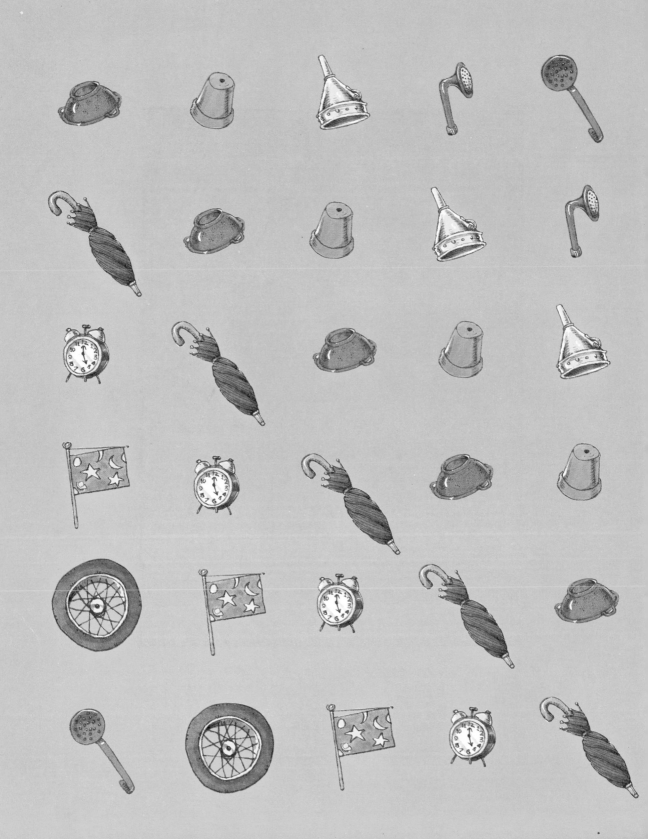

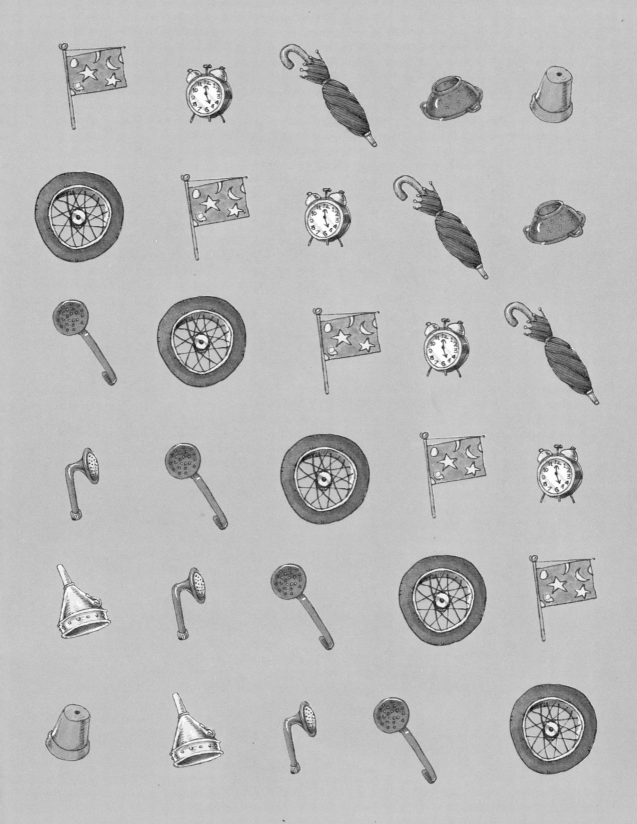

For Françoise
C. Mc.

First published 1981 by
Walker Books Ltd
87 Vauxhall Walk
London SE11 5HJ

This edition published 1989

Text © 1981 Russell Hoban
Illustrations © 1981 Colin McNaughton

Printed in Italy by Lito di Roberto Terrazzi

British Library Cataloguing in Publication Data
Hoban, Russell, *1925-*
They came from Aargh!
I. Title   II. McNaughton, Colin
813′.54[J]
ISBN 0-7445-1211-5

THEY CAME FROM AARGH!

Written by

Russell Hoban

Illustrated by

Colin McNaughton

WALKER BOOKS
LONDON

They came from Aargh!
They came from Ugh!
They came from beyond the galaxy.
All of them were alien, all of them were strange.

Their ship was strange and alien, it had
twelve legs.
Their battle cry was, "Three chairs for Aargh!
Three chairs for Ugh!"

Commander Blob read out the readout on the big display.

He read, "Zom! Zeem! Plovsnat! Ruk!"

Navigator Blub was taking a star sight.

"Ruk at fifteen point vom," he said. "Plovsnat
at thirty-seven zeems and holding vummitch."
"Vummitch it is," said Commander Blob.
"I'm taking her in."

Technician Bleep was on the scanner.
"What do you scan?" said Blob.
"Cay!" said Bleep. "Chah!"
"Chocolate cake," said Blub.
"Prepare to land," said Blob.

"Four legs down," said Blub. "Eight legs down. Twelve legs down."

"Jets on full, jets on half, jets on quarter, we're down," said Blob.

Ssssss! went the airlock, and out they came,
moving slowly, moving carefully, looking all
round slowly and carefully.
They had their bimblers ready, they had their
globsters on as well, they had their cake
beam going.
"Is there intelligent life on this planet?" said Blub.

"Nobody knows," said Blob. "Keep your globster
and your bimbler ready, we don't know what we
might run into."

"Chah!" said Bleep.

Bzzzzzzzt! Bzzzzzzzt! went the cake beam.

"He's beaming us into the chocolate cake,"
said Blob.

"Look out," said Blub, "there's something coming."

"What is it?" said Blob.

"It's shocking and horrible," said Blub.

"It's a shock horror," said Blob.

"It has seven heads and five wings," said Blub.

"It's flying in a circle," said Blob.

"That's because it has three wings on one side
and two on the other," said Blub.
"It's an asymmetrical shock horror," said Blob.
"We'd better bimble it before it bimbles us."
"Let's try giving it some milk," said Blub.
"It may be friendly."

They gave the asymmetrical shock horror
some milk. It purred as it lapped it up.
"Put that in your report," said Blob to Blub.
"Blub reporting to base," said Blub into

his helmet radio. "Asymmetrical shock horror
fond of milk, purrs."

"Let's press on," said Blob. "I want to finish up
here and get back to Aargh! and Ugh! before dark."

"How long will it take us to get back?" said Blub. "Seventy-five jars," said Blob. "But if we go into hyperjam we can make it three times as sticky." "We'd better hyperjam it out of here then," said Blub. "There's something big coming this way."

"Is it intelligent life?" said Blob.

"It's a mummosaurus," said Blub.

"Great blubbering blue blibbles!" said Blob.

"What's it going to do?"

"Cheese omelettes," said the mummosaurus,
"with chips and baked beans."
"Careful," said Blob to Blub and Bleep, "this
may be a trap."
"Chah! Chah! Chah!" said Bleep, stamping
his feet and dancing about.

"You can't have chocolate cake until you've eaten your cheese omelette," said the mummosaurus.

The mummosaurus put the cheese omelettes on the table.

"Looks pretty good actually," said Blob.

"The mummosaurus is attacking the ship!" said
Blub. "It's tearing it apart," said Blob.
"What shall we do?" said Blub.
"Eat our cheese omelettes," said Blob, "and wait
for a chance to escape."

"In what?" said Blub. "We've got no ship now."
"Don't panic," said Blob. "Maybe we can do a deal."
"Right you are," said the mummosaurus. "Eat
your omelettes and your beans and chips and
then you can have your chocolate cake and then
you can put your space ship back together."

"Chah!" said Bleep.

"That's it," said the mummosaurus. "Chocolate cake all round."

When Blob and Blub and Bleep had finished

they thanked the mummosaurus.

"You're very welcome," said the mummosaurus.
"Drop in any time you're in this part of the
solar system."

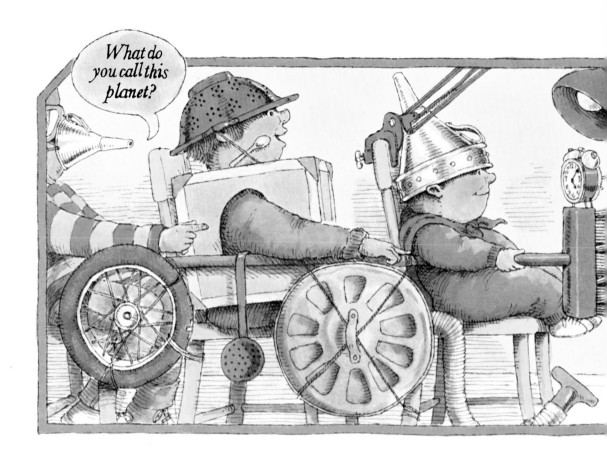

"What do you call this planet?" said Blob when they had the space ship back together and were ready to blast off.

"We call it Earth," said the mummosaurus.

"What do you call it?"

"We call it Plovsnat," said Blob. "In our language that means the place of chocolate cake."

"Ready for blastoff," said Blub.

Everybody kissed the mummosaurus goodbye.
"Blast off!" said Blob.
Off they blasted, roaring into space, and as they
set their course for home they shouted their new
battle cry,

"Three chahs for Aargh! Three chahs for Ugh!"

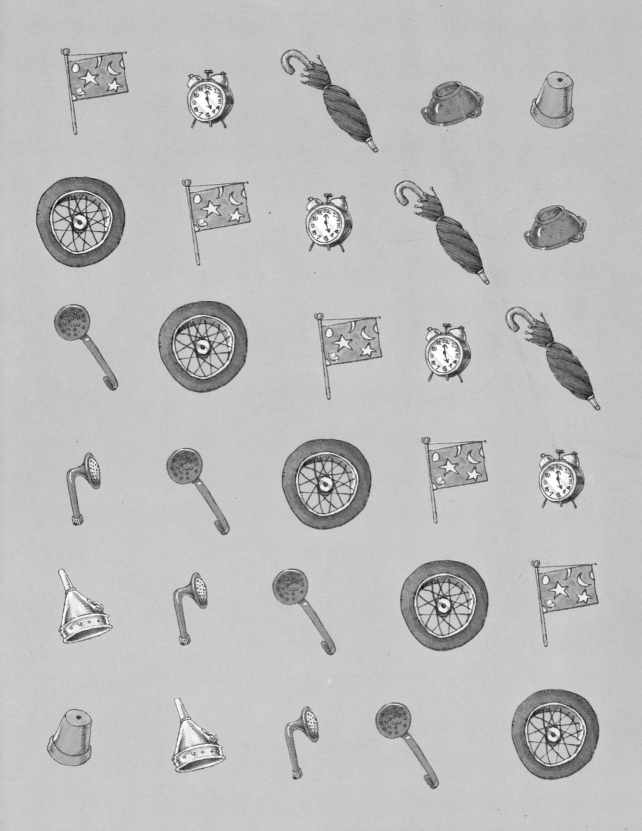

MORE WALKER PAPERBACKS

THE PRE-SCHOOL YEARS

**John Satchwell
& Katy Sleight**
Monster Maths
ODD ONE OUT   BIG AND LITTLE
COUNTING   SHAPES

FOR THE VERY YOUNG

Byron Barton
TRAINS   TRUCKS   BOATS
AEROPLANES

PICTURE BOOKS
For All Ages

Colin West
"HELLO, GREAT BIG BULLFROG!"
"PARDON?" SAID THE GIRAFFE
"HAVE YOU SEEN THE CROCODILE?"
"NOT ME," SAID THE MONKEY

Bob Graham
THE RED WOOLLEN BLANKET

**Russell Hoban
& Colin McNaughton**
The Hungry Three
THEY CAME FROM AARGH!
THE GREAT FRUIT GUM ROBBERY

Jill Murphy
FIVE MINUTES' PEACE

**Philippa Pearce
& John Lawrence**
EMILY'S OWN ELEPHANT

**David Lloyd
& Charlotte Voake**
THE RIDICULOUS STORY OF
GAMMER GURTON'S NEEDLE

Nicola Bayley
Copycats
SPIDER CAT   PARROT CAT
POLAR BEAR CAT   ELEPHANT CAT
CRAB CAT

**Michael Rosen
& Quentin Blake**
Scrapbooks
SMELLY JELLY SMELLY JELLY
(THE SEASIDE BOOK)

HARD-BOILED LEGS
(THE BREAKFAST BOOK)

SPOLLYOLLYDIDDLYTIDDLYITIS
(THE DOCTOR BOOK)

UNDER THE BED
(THE BEDTIME BOOK)

Jan Ormerod
THE STORY OF CHICKEN LICKEN

**Bamber Gascoigne
& Joseph Wright**
BOOK OF AMAZING FACTS 1

Martin Handford
WHERE'S WALLY?